Fly Anyway

By Kelly Jo Terry, Illustrator
& Amy Quezon-Wilde, Author

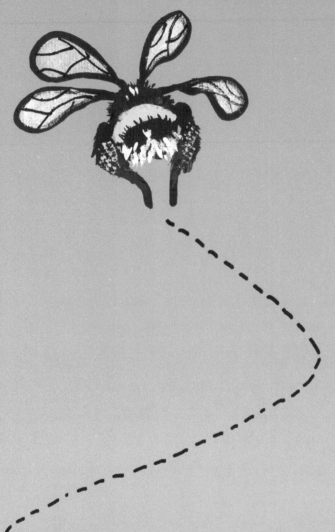

Published by Richter Publishing LLC www.richterpublishing.com

Illustrations: Kelly Jo Terry

Editors: Brianna Miranda -Solberg

Book Formatting: Tara Richter

ISBN: 978-1-954094-36-9 Hardback

U.S. Library of Congress Registration & Copyright Number: (coming soon)

Dedication

This book is dedicated to all of the children we have
ever loved, but especially to our Sammy, without whom
Bea would not be.

Introduction

Legend has it, there is a quote that hangs in the halls of NASA that reads, "Aerodynamically a bumble bee's body is not made to fly because the breadth of its wings is too small to keep its huge body in flight. The good thing is, the bee doesn't know that and flies anyway."

This sweet tale tells the story of one such bee. On her very first day in her very own garden Beatrix Bernadette Bellarosa sets off on a journey that has her buzzing far and wide to meet all sorts of flying creatures. She's got big dreams but the friends she meets along the way, aren't always so sure. Through resiliency and determination, and with a little encouragement from a sweet friend, Bea completes her adventure and learns the lesson of a lifetime... believe in yourself and fly anyway.

There once was a bee named Beatrix Bernadette Bellarosa, but everyone just called her Bea. She was brilliant and bold and wanted to fly more than anything in the world.

On her very first day in her very own garden, she met Butterfly.

"Hello," said Bea to Butterfly, "my name is Bea and I want to fly!"

"Oh, Bea," Butterfly said resting on a delicate stem, "you can't fly. Your wings are not colorful like mine."

This news made Bea very sad, and she began to cry.

Bea's friend Flower saw that Bea was crying. "Why are you so sad?" asked Flower.

"Because I want to fly, but Butterfly says I can't because my wings aren't colorful enough."

"Well," said Flower, "there are lots of creatures that fly. Why don't you go and ask some of them?"

So that is exactly what Bea decided to do.

First, Bea buzzed to the beach and there she met Albatross.

"Hello," said Bea to Albatross, "my name is Bea and I want to fly."

"Oh Bea," squawked Albatross, standing on the warm sandy beach, "you can't fly. Your wings are not big like mine."

This was not the news that Bea wanted to hear, so she decided to go ask someone else.

Next, Bea buzzed out to sea, where she met Flying Fish.

"Hello," said Bea to Flying Fish, "my name is Bea and I want to fly."

"Oh Bea," bubbled Flying Fish, splashing in the cool, rolling waves, "you can't fly. You don't have shimmering fins to launch you into the air like I do."

Once again, Bea was not happy with this news, so she decided to keep going and buzzed to the city where she met Pigeon.

"Hello," said Bea to Pigeon, "my name is Bea and I want to fly."

"Oh Bea," cooed Pigeon, balancing on a very high wire, "you can't fly. You don't have fluffy feathers like I do."

Disappointed with this news, Bea decided to venture on.

This time, Bea buzzed down to a farm and there she met Owl.

"Hello," said Bea to Owl, "my name is Bea and I want to fly."

"Ssshhh," whispered Owl, resting on a nest made of straw, "I'm sleeping."

"But it's the middle of the day," said Bea.

"That's when owls sleep," said the drowsy bird. "Clearly, you can't fly because you don't know enough. You're not wise yet, like I am."

Unhappy with this opinion, but not wanting to give up, Bea kept going.

Filled with determination, Bea buzzed to the mountains, where she met Eagle.

"Hello," said Bea to Eagle, "my name is Bea and I want to fly."

"Oh Bea," declared Eagle, majestically perched on a giant boulder, "you can't fly. You're not strong and powerful like I am."

Getting sadder by the moment, but determined to be brave and bold, Bea buzzed on.

Carefully, Bea buzzed into a spooky dark cave, where she met Bat.

"Hello," said Bea to Bat, "my name is Bea and I want to fly."

"Oh Bea," squeaked Bat, hanging upside down in the dusky cave, "you can't fly. You don't have bones in your wings like I do."

Tears welling up in her eyes, but not wanting to quit, Bea buzzed her way to the desert, where she met Hummingbird.

"Hello," said Bea to Hummingbird, "my name is Bea and I want to fly."

"Oh Bea," peeped Hummingbird, fluttering near a cactus flower, "you can't fly, your body is too big for your tiny wings. You're not dainty like I am."

Growing more and more disappointed, Bea decided to ask just one more creature.

Gathering her energy, Bea buzzed all the way down to the jungle, where she met Toucan.

"Hello," said Bea to Toucan, "my name is Bea and I want to fly."

"Oh Bea," said Toucan, clinging to a twisty branch, "you can't fly. You don't have a big bright beak like I do."

And with that, Beatrix Bernadette Bellarosa became the saddest bee to ever be. So, she went back to her garden, snuggled into Flower, and cried and cried and cried.

"Oh Bea," said Flower, "what happened? You look like the saddest bee to ever be."

"I am," sniffed Bea. "I want to fly more than anything in the whole wide world, but I can't."

"Why not?" asked Flower.

"Because... Butterfly said my wings aren't colorful enough. Albatross said my wings are not big enough. Flying Fish said I don't have strong, shimmering fins. Pigeon said I don't have feathers.

Owl said I'm not wise enough. Eagle said I'm not powerful enough. Bat said I don't have bones in my wings. Hummingbird said my body is too big. And Toucan said I don't have a bright beak."

"My goodness," said Flower, "that's a lot of friends! How ever did you visit them all?"

"Well," whimpered Bea, "I... I... I flew."

Surprised and very happy with the words she'd just said, Bea said them again, but louder this time.

"I flew! I flew! I really flew!" Bea shouted as she zoomed around her garden.

"Yes, yes you did, Bea!" exclaimed Flower "You see it
really doesn't matter what anyone says about you.

"Just believe in yourself and fly anyway."

So as a very tired Bea FLEW home...

that's exactly what she decided to do.

About the Authors

Amy and Kelly have been friends for more than 25 years and have been there for each other, through all the ups and downs that come with raising kids. It was during one of the most difficult times that the story of "Bea" slowly came to life. Bea's soulful determination, along with the steadfast and loving patience of her friend "Flower," shows us what we are all capable of when we believe in ourselves.

Kelly Jo Terry

Kelly Jo Terry is an artist and writer who lives with her husband, their big, blended family and her beloved pup Jaates in Tampa, FL. From her tiny home studio, overlooking her two apiaries, she created and painted Bea and all of the flying friends she meets on the journey to believing in herself

Amy Quezon-Wilde

Amy Quezon-Wilde is a mother of four, lawyer and adjunct law professor who lives in Tampa, Florida with her husband and family. She hopes you love Bea's story of hope and resiliency.

Printed in the USA
CPSIA information can be obtained
at www.ICGtesting.com
JSHW040043031023
49200JS00024B/55